GAMER

First published in 2012 in Great Britain by
Barrington Stoke Ltd
18 Walker Street, Edinburgh, EH3 7LP

This edition published 2015

Adapted from a story previously published as
Virtual Kombat, Puffin, 2010

www.barringtonstoke.co.uk

A CIP catalogue record for this book is available from the British
Library upon request

ISBN: 978-1-78112-477-2

Printed in China by Leo

Warning: Do not attempt any of the techniques described within
this book without the supervision of a qualified instructor. These
can be highly dangerous moves and result in fatal injuries. The
author and the publisher take no responsibility for any injuries
resulting from attempting these techniques.

GAMER

Chris Bradford

Barrington Stoke

For Matt, a loyal friend

CONTENTS

CHAPTER 1
Bread

I can't tear my eyes away from the fighters.

Thunderbolt the kick-boxer has just knocked Destroy's front teeth out. Destroy reels from the blow, spits blood. He is a powerful heavyweight boxer. He puts his head down like a bull and charges at Thunderbolt. His anvil-sized fist drives into Thunderbolt's gut. Thunderbolt collapses. Next, Destroy catches him with an upper hook on the chin. Thunderbolt's whole body flips high into the air, then lands in a dazed pile in the centre of the Arena.

The crowd jeer and shout.

I hold my breath. Thunderbolt was the favourite to win this match.

Destroy raises his fists on either side of Thunderbolt's head and slams them together. It's his most famous move – the Skull Crusher.

It's Game Over for Thunderbolt.

The 3D Street Screen in front of me switches to a red and black logo –

VK

A deep voice growls, "VIRTUAL KOMBAT. SO REAL IT HURTS."

After that an advert comes on for Synapse drinks, the main company that sponsors Virtual Kombat. I try not to look. Adverts just make me want what I can't have.

Now the fight is over, the street kids turn away. They drift into the side alleys with the rest of the rubbish that pollutes this city. Unwanted. Ignored. Forgotten.

I'm one of them. Scott. Just another stray on the streets.

I lost my parents to the killer virus of 2030. It wiped out millions. Only thing was, it didn't seem to affect kids. At one point, docs said it might be *us* spreading the virus. Some parents even dumped their own kids on the streets. The orphans ended up there too. Now there are thousands of us.

The whole world went to pot. Then the army took over and their tough new laws brought order to the place. After that, people stopped going outside. The virus had run its course by then, but adults were still scared they might catch something. Most people escaped into life on the net. That's when VK first started. People needed an outlet – something to funnel all their anger and despair into.

VIRTUAL KOMBAT
The most realistic fighting game ever!

That's what the ads say. Virtual Kombat is *the* Number 1 show in the world. Everyone watches or plays. Massive Street Screens are everywhere in the city. Like sick suns that never set.

On the screen in front of me, a huge 3D picture of a Zing energy bar appears. I turn away. It's torture.

I hear a blast of horns and pounding drums. It's the VK theme tune. The ad break is over and the logo returns. The voice is back too – "THE MOST REALISTIC FIGHT GAME EVER. WHERE EVERY ENEMY HAS A MIND OF ITS OWN."

Two air-brushed presenters appear on the screen and flash their shiny white teeth. It's Highlight Time – all today's deaths repeated on a screen ten storeys high. Heads chopped off, limbs crushed, kombatants killed. They show every gory detail.

The leader-board flashes up. Destroy has jumped one place. Thunderbolt's name is gone.

VIRTUAL KOMBAT. SO REAL IT HURTS.

The only thing that hurts me at the moment is my stomach. I haven't eaten in days. VK takes my mind off the hunger. When the show's on, you don't think about it so much. But when it's over, the emptiness grips my guts once more.

I can't face the re-runs, and so I head up a narrow backstreet. There are big dumpbins down here, behind the restaurants where the rich and powerful eat. They still go out. That's if you count sealed MPVs, glass-covered walkways and huge malls as 'outside'.

If I'm lucky, I might find a few scraps thrown out by the chefs into the bins.

Then I hear a voice. "Hand it over!"

In the gloom up ahead, I see two lads standing over a little girl and boy.

The girl shakes her blonde head and hugs a brown paper bag closer to her chest. The taller of the two lads slaps her hard across the face and rips the bag from her grasp.

The girl doesn't cry. Street kids are tough. But even from here I can see the red mark of a hand-print on her cheek.

"Leave my sis alone," yells the boy, as he steps between them. "Give that back. It's *ours!*"

"Finders keepers, losers weepers," the other lad mocks. He's stocky, with dark red hair. He shoves the boy to the ground and laughs as the kid cracks his head on the kerb.

"You won't believe this, Juice," says the taller lad. His eyes glow with pleasure. "They've got bread."

CHAPTER 2
Street Fighter

My stomach growls. What I'd do for bread.

"Give us a bite, Stick," the lad called Juice demands.

Stick holds the bag out of reach. "No way!"

"Aw, come on," Juice pleads. "The others won't know if a bit's gone."

While they argue, I creep up behind them and grab the bread.

"Oi!" snarls Stick, as he spins round in shock. "That's ours!"

"Finders keepers, losers weepers," I say. I show no fear. Fear is what gets you killed in this city.

Stick and Juice are just bullies who pick on smaller kids. So I'm not scared.

But I'm taking a gamble. It's still two against one.

"This wasn't yours to begin with," I say, with a glare. "Now zap off!"

With a worried glance at Stick, Juice backs away. But Stick pulls a broken pipe from his belt.

Looks like I lost the bet.

Stick takes a wild swing at my head. I drop the bread and dart forward to double-block his attack. Then I drag his arm into a lock that forces him to drop the pipe in pain. Juice jumps on me from behind and tries to choke me. I elbow him in the ribs. He lets go and I fling him over my shoulder. As he lands, I punch him in the guts.

Stick pulls the gasping Juice to his feet. "Wait till Shark hears about this," Stick says. "He'll blaze and burn you!"

I stand my ground as they limp away. But inside I'm screaming at myself. "*IDIOT!*"

Shark's not someone you want to cross. Not even for a bag of bread. He's got a bad rep. But how was I to know that his guys would be in this zone? This is Bleeder turf. It doesn't make sense for Shark's guys to be scouting for food here. They must be new to this game.

As I reach down to pick up the bag, I find I am swaying. The effort of the fight has made me even weaker. I need food.

The little girl and boy shiver with cold and hunger. The drizzle of rain never stops in this city. They cling to each other and stare at me. It's clear they're twins. Blond hair. Baby blue eyes. And they have a look of fear and sadness that breaks my heart.

"What are your names?" I ask.

"Mine's Tommy. My sis is Tammy," the boy blurts out.

As hungry as I am, I hand the little girl back the bag of bread. "Well, this is yours, Tammy."

She says nothing, but hugs the bag to her chest.

"Who are you?" Tommy whispers, his eyes wide with shock.

Kindness is a rare thing on these streets. It's a dumb thing too, I tell myself. I could starve.

"Scott," I say.

"Where did you learn to fight like that?" Tommy asks.

"*Street Fighter 7.*"

I smile as the memory washes over me.

It's true. Before the virus, I lived in a great house on the south side of the city. My parents were ace. Got me everything I wanted. The top games console, the latest games. My dad and I were hooked on *Street Fighter*. I used to try out some of the moves on him for real. I never won. He was ex-SAS and a black belt in *tae kwon do*. We trained together every day. That training is one of the reasons I'm still around, when so many others aren't.

I shake my head and focus on the here and now. Tammy is opening the bag. Her eyes dart around the alley, like a mouse ready to run at the first sign of danger.

"She doesn't say much, your sis," I say to Tommy.

Tommy shakes his head.

My mouth waters as Tammy pulls out a large hunk of bread. She passes the bag to me without a word and rips off half of her own share to give to Tommy. I look in the bag. She's left me more than half. I'm too hungry even to thank her. I devour it.

"This bread's fresh!" I say, my mouth full.

Tommy nods. "The cook always makes a little extra for us. It has boosters in."

I lose myself in the nutty crust and soft inside of the bread. Already I can feel my strength return as the energy boosters in the food do their work.

I finish it all too soon and wipe my mouth on my sleeve. "That was great."

Tammy smiles for the first time.

Then, just as fast, her smile is gone.

"THERE HE IS!"

I spin round. Stick and Juice stand at the end of the alley, pointing at me. This time they have the whole Shark gang as back-up. Shark himself is in front. He wears a black leather jacket and has a spike of ice-blond hair. He grins at me. No need to guess how *he* got his name. Two rows of broken teeth glint in the glow of the Street Screens.

Shark pulls a Blazer from his pocket and flicks on its pulse-blade.

It's fight or flight time.

I run.

CHAPTER 3
Roof Escape

Their feet pound after me as I duck down a narrow side street. I know this city zone like the back of my hand and I take a short-cut onto Main Street. I dodge sleek, shiny MPVs as I shoot across the road into the alley on the other side. But I can't shake Shark's gang off.

They're closing on me fast. I can hear Shark cursing me.

I have to make a roof escape.

As I run round a corner, I spot what I need. I leap onto a dumpbin and launch myself into the air. My hands catch hold of the bottom rung of a fire-escape ladder and I pull myself up. I climb and climb, until I reach the roof, 12 floors up. Far below me is the grid of the city, laid out in lights. A vast metal forest of Street Screens, TV dishes and mobile masts sprout from the roof tops in every direction.

Down below, the gang have split up. Shark and several others follow me. The rest scurry like rats along the maze of alleys. They crane their necks to see me gap-jump to the next roof.

I land and roll. Without stopping, I speed-jump an air shaft and sprint across to the next building. This time the jump is much bigger. I do it anyway. Fear and booster bread give me strength. But the drop knocks the breath out of me. I hit the roof hard, and slam into the legs of a Street Screen.

As I look up, the words "VINCE POWER – CAN HE SAVE OUR CITY?" are beamed onto the screen. A clean-cut, tanned man in a crisp blue suit appears. His silver-grey hair only adds to his charm. I don't need to read his name to know who he is. He's one of the richest and most powerful men in the world. He invented VK.

I sit up and see Juice attempt the leap I have just made.

But he doesn't make it.

As he slams into the roof edge, Juice's face is a mask of horror. He tries to cling on and I think about saving him, but Shark's already across. He ignores Juice and races after me.

I drop down to a lower roof and flee.

Shark stays high and we race side by side on different buildings.

He's fast and I have to use all my skill to stay ahead.

Far below in the alleys, I catch snatches of his gang watching me in the hope I fall. Then I lose sight of Shark and I think *he's* fallen.

But then I see the leather jacket and the spiked hair appear in front of me. My way is blocked. I back off. Stick lands behind me with a thud.

My only escape now is the building to my right. But the roof is a long way down.

Shark grins from ear to ear as he pulls out his Blazer.

"Time to blaze and burn!" he says.

I've got no choice. I *have* to make the leap.

I dash to the edge of the roof and throw myself into the void. For a few seconds the air seems to take my weight as I plummet down. Then I crash onto the tar roof of the other building. I grunt in pain as my foot twists under me.

Stick stares across the huge gap in shock. He won't be following me.

Then a shadow flies through the air and Shark lands next to me. He crashes head first into a TV dish. The boy's crazier than I am – and I had no choice!

Pain shoots up my leg as I limp away. I see on a Street Screen that the interview with Vince Power has begun.

"Many people think you're a hero," the presenter lady simpers. She's all fake eyelashes and plastic surgery. "Your VK program has cut violent crime, and your company Power Inc. pays for the City Orphans' Home," she goes on. "What drives a man like you?"

Vince Power smiles. "I believe in the greatest good for the greatest number. I offer a way out for these kids. Hope in a hopeless world."

I turn away from the Screen. Shark's back on his feet. He strides over to me.

I'm trapped against the mobile mast. I'm hurt – and I have no way to escape.

There's a sharp buzz as Shark's pulse-blade lights up.

"No hope for you now, pretty boy," he snarls, and he points the Blazer at my face.

At that moment, the tinkly tune of an ice-cream van drifts up from below.

Shark freezes. We both know what that means.

"I'll blaze you later," he says and snaps off the laser.

CHAPTER 4
Selector Truck

As I hobble into the square, I see I'm too late.

A mass of street kids crowds a massive white truck with the VK logo painted along its side. The ice-cream van tune stops. All the free Zing bars have been given out and the PlayPods are full.

I swear. Just my luck. The very night I get jumped on, the VK Selector Truck visits *our* zone!

The truck is the one way to get off these streets. It's a mobile VK game station. If you can prove you're good enough, you become a games tester for Vince Power. That gets you a place in his City Orphans' Home. Food every day, a soft bed, heating, school – a chance at a normal life.

Even if they don't choose you, you still get a food pack. That makes all the difference on the streets – you can eat and trade. Survive.

But I missed out.

Shark didn't. He's in the black leather seat of a PlayPod, with his mind-control headset in place. His gang push and shove to get a better view of his Play Screen. Then Stick spots me in the crowd.

I decide not to hang around. Whether Shark becomes a tester or not, we have a score to settle and his gang will still be after me. I'll have to move to a new zone.

As I limp away, I hear my name.

Tommy's in a PlayPod. He waves at me to come over.

"Take my place," he says.

"What?" I say. "Are you crazy? Chances like this don't come every day."

Tommy looks at the mute girl standing beside me. "I can't leave me sis behind, can I?"

He scoots off his seat. "I was saving it for you, anyway."

"KOMBATANTS READY!" booms a voice through the truck's speakers.

There's no time to argue. I clamber in as fast as I can. Just as I pull down the headset, the game begins.

CHAPTER 5
Game Over

My brain goes dark.

Flashes of light streak past my eyes and in a heart-beat I'm transported to an exotic Chinese temple. Stone dragons fill each corner of the chamber, their mouths brimming with fire. Steel spikes stick up from the floorboards in a large ring – the edge of the fight zone.

This is a single-room Arena, made for training. No exits. No puzzles. And no enemy or monsters. Just fighter-versus-fighter kombat. An all-out knock-down match where only the last survivor wins.

The other kombatants stand in a circle, waiting for the command to begin.

I flick my eyes to the right and inspect the choices for my avatar. There's not much left. A sumo wrestler. A girl ninja. An old priest. Then

I see the familiar white jacket of a *tae kwon do* master. My body morphs from the default setting into the strong, lean build of a martial arts expert.

My avatar's green life-bar flashes up in my lower vision.

It's been a while since I played a video game. Could do with some practice.

VK's changed gaming almost beyond recognition. No more jumping around your living room with a controller that never registers fast enough on screen. Not since Vince Power invented mind-control headsets. Hoodies, we call them. You just think your actions and they happen on screen. Then, last year, the sets were upgraded with a direct link into the brain. Gamers now *live* the game – in their heads!

A blast of horns is replaced with pounding Japanese drums.

"KOMMENCE KOMBAT!"

The Arena turns into a bloody free-for-all. Twenty kids fight for one place in the Orphans'

Home. I glance around, wondering which kid is Shark.

A warrior princess is hurled through the air. Blood gushes out of her chest as she's skewered on a floor spike. A huge African wrestler hammers a soldier-of-fortune into the ground. In the same second, a man in dark shades and a long black leather jacket destroys a Shaolin monk with a lethal series of flying kicks.

A tattooed Mongol warrior towers over me and takes a brutal swing with a club. But he misses by a mile.

A bit of luck. My first opponent must be new to gaming. He can hardly control his avatar, and he's wide open to attack. I fell him with a lightning-fast sweep-kick. Then I pummel him with a rapid flurry of punches – each one making a gut-churning crunch in the game's sound effects. His life-bar blinks out as I finish him off with an axe-kick. The warrior spews up virtual blood.

Since I know my avatar's fighting style, I can react faster than the others and inflict high-damage blows. In seconds I take out a samurai warrior, a Thai kick-boxer and the African wrestler.

I feel my pulse racing as the kombat adrenaline pumps through me. It's like the real thing – but without the pain.

Only a few kombatants left.

The one I think of as 'Leatherman', now makes his way towards me. This avatar moves well and looks dangerous. He whirls in the air and spin-kicks me in the jaw. I reel as stars flash before my eyes. My life-bar flickers and I lose a health point. He follows up with a series of roundhouse-kicks and back-kicks. My life-bar drops again and again. It becomes harder and harder to control my avatar.

80% ... 60% ... 45% ... 30% ...

My vision's now blurry and red flashes dance in my eyes. I can't take much more damage.

I flip away as an Amazonian warrior attacks Leatherman from behind. She's the only other kombatant left. That's until Leatherman jumps up and catches her head between his legs. He breaks her neck with a double-twist.

As I watch him destroy the Amazonian, I realise something. All Leatherman can do is kick.

I back away to the edge of the ring and slump as if defeated. I want to bait him to come in to finish me. To end the game.

He executes a flying side-kick. At the same time, I drop and slide beneath him. Outwitted, Leatherman can't stop himself and lands on the deadly spikes. Somewhere in the background, beyond the game itself, I'm aware of distant cheering.

GAME OVER

My vision goes blank.

I pull off the hoody, blinking as my eyes adjust to the real world. For a moment, I can't process where I am. I feel sick, as if I've been spun round too much.

The crowd's cheering me as Shark is escorted off the truck. He has his consolation prize of a food pack in hand. He doesn't look very consoled.

He snatches his leather jacket from Stick and glares up at me.

"I'll blaze you one day," he growls.

In his hand, the pulse-blade of his Blazer flashes on and off.

As the truck begins to drive away, I spy Tommy and his sister among the mass of shouting kids. I throw him my food pack.

He grins and gives me a good-luck 'V' sign. Then he flips it to the side to make a 'K'.

CHAPTER 6
Kat-Ana

"Welcome to your new home," says the tall, silver-haired charm that is Vince Power.

He flashes a pearly white smile. Everyone beams back. It's like a dream for us 15 new kids gathered in the main hall of the Vince Power City Orphans' Home. The building is all fancy arches and glass-domes in the roof.

Since I got here, I've had a medical check-up, my first wash in weeks and I've slept in a proper bed. I've eaten hot food and been given new clothes – an all-black kombat suit with the VK logo in red on the chest. My name is laser-stitched in white across the back –

SCOTT

I was supposed to choose a name for my avatar tag. But I couldn't think of a good one at the time.

"You've all shown a natural talent for VK," explains Vince Power. "You're here to develop those skills and become game testers for the next generation of VK. All I ask in return is that you obey the rules."

A tall black girl with the tag VIXEN puts her hand up. "What *are* the rules?"

Vince looks at her, his face grave. Then grins. "There aren't any."

Everyone laughs.

"Not in the Arena, at least. But here, the guardians will look after you."

He points to a row of 30 or so men and women, all looking sharp in red VK uniforms. A large, round-faced woman shoots me a friendly wink. The rest look a bit severe and military for my liking.

"All we ask is respect," Power says. "For your own safety, please don't wander into any restricted areas. Stay within the Orphans' Home. And go to bed at lights out."

A groan echoes through the hall. Vince Power ignores it. He sweeps his hand round to indicate the huge room, large enough to seat 500. "This is where you'll eat," he says. "Breakfast, lunch and dinner."

I gasp in amazement with the other kids. *Three* meals a day?

Above us, on the main wall, a huge screen shows the daily VK Grand Arena show. Destroy's on air again. He's entered the Warrior Top Ten, because he's just beaten Chaos in a Face-off. Chaos's brains are splattered all over the screen, another victim of Destroy's Skull Crusher move.

"Through the glass doors is the Chill Zone," explains Vince, with a nod and a smile at Destroy's gory victory. "It's the place you can relax after training. Follow me."

This room's kitted out with sofas, beanbags, vending machines and PlayPods. A bunch of kids are chilling out in one corner. They salute Vince as he enters, but they don't even give us a glance. Their eyes are fixed on a grid of smaller screens on the far wall. Different Arenas are being broadcast from the one in the dining hall.

A digital leader-board displays the names of kombatants I've never heard of. Even Destroy is missing from the Top Ten.

"Which VK League is this?" I ask.

"Your one," says Vince. "These are feeds from the Training Zone. You can watch your fellow kombatants fighting at any time."

On the central screen a girl avatar is battling a ninja assassin. She reminds me of a retro Lara Croft in her shorts and tight T-shirt, a samurai sword strapped to her back. The display flashes –

GINGER NINJA vs KAT-ANA

The Ginger Ninja leaps through the air, twisting and kicking like a lightning bolt. He's so fast that it's all I can do to keep my eyes on him. But Kat-Ana slips away from every attack. All of a sudden, she power-drives upwards and catches the flying ninja from below with a strike that makes my eyes water.

Ginger Ninja slumps to the ground. Taking her time, Kat-Ana launches herself and lands two massive elbow strikes to the head. The ninja's eyeballs pop out of his skull.

"KILLING STRIKE!"

A fanfare of horns ends the match. In seconds the kids in the corner have drowned it out with a storm of jeers and shouts. Kat-Ana's name jumps one place on the leader-board to 9.

"The top-scoring kombatant each week is promoted to Elite Gamer status and goes through to our Special Projects Area," explains Vince. "Those who excel in Special Projects then enter the Grand Arena – a chance to fight for the VK Crown itself."

Frantic whispers spread among the new arrivals. The Crown is the ultimate prize. £10 million, plus your name in the Warrior Hall of Fame.

Vince leads us down a hallway lit with neon lights to a door marked "TRAINING ZONE". We enter a large round room. Three men in white VK uniforms are at a control module in the centre, studying banks of mini screens.

"These are the Analysts," Vince tells us. "They assess every fight, give feedback and select your training programmes. As you hone your VK skills, you test our games to the limit."

I gaze in amazement at the hundreds of doors that surround us on three levels. All have a number, apart from a single lower one with a "RESTRICTED ACCESS" sign.

"Your PlayPods are all separate," a pasty-faced Analyst explains. "That way we can monitor your real *and* virtual selves in a controlled environment."

Door 36 opens with a soft swish. I look over and see a girl with a bob of jet-black hair, a nose-stud and black eyeliner come out. As she walks up to the desk, I read the tag on her back – KAT-ANA. She's kinda cute, but no Lara Croft.

A moment later, a door on Level 2 slides open. A mop of bright orange hair blunders out. Under it is a tiny boy, his face red, eyes bloodshot. This must be the Ginger Ninja.

"That's not fair!" the boy shouts at Kat-Ana. "You punched me in the – Oh! Mr Power."

The Ginger Ninja salutes Vince and then walks stiffly down the stairs to the central desk. As Kat-Ana finishes her debrief, Vince calls her over.

"One of our rising stars," he says, and lays a proud hand on her back.

She nods coolly at us.

Vince's blue eyes sparkle. "Anyone brave enough to go up against her?"

CHAPTER 7
Pain Limiter

My father's SAS motto was "WHO DARES WINS".

I'm not one to back down myself, no matter what the odds.

I step forward.

Door 12 slides open and I clamber into a silver PlayPod.

Vince Power and an Analyst join me in the room.

"What are these for?" I ask as the Analyst belts me into the seat with velcro straps.

"This is a new generation VK system," the Analyst says. "Your brain won't be able to tell what's real and what isn't. Until you're used to VK2, your mind could instruct your *real* body, as well as the avatar's. The straps are just for safety."

I frown and look to Vince, who nods.

"Any problems, press the red ESCAPE button on your avatar's belt," he says, fixing me with his perfect smile. "It cuts the link to the VK server on the spot."

A red scanner passes across my face. The hoody slips down. I see a jolt of light and feel a sense of falling.

My breath is taken away as a forest bursts into life before my eyes.

The Arena is so vivid. So *real*. I can hear birds singing and leaves rustling. I smell pine trees and spring flowers. I even feel a cool breeze on my face.

It's freaky. Like being in a dream. In another dream.

I look down and am comforted to see the red pulse of the VK ESCAPE button on my belt. This is the gameworld.

Kat-Ana's waiting for me, her sword slung across her back. Close up, her avatar's face looks just like hers. Mine must be the same. Our features scanned on to the computer characters.

"Forgot our shirt, did we?" she asks as she strolls over.

I glance down at my chest and admire my rippling six-pack and toned muscles. I wear loose fighting slacks and black sneakers.

Without warning, Kat-Ana kicks me in the stomach.

I double up, winded. An upper-cut from Kat-Ana floors me. Searing pain rockets through my skull and I taste blood. In a blind panic, I stab at the ESCAPE button.

The forest shrinks to a tiny dot. Then blinks out.

As the hoody comes off, I gasp, "Something's wrong. I felt pain."

Vince grins at me. "Surely you've seen the advert?"

I remember.

SO REAL IT HURTS

"*This* is what makes VK2 the most realistic fighting game ever," Vince says. "You feel both the thrill of the fight *and* the pain."

I rub my jaw where there's a dull throb.

"Your body's not damaged, but you may feel some after-effects as your brain readjusts," the Analyst informs me. He is checking my pulse. "This soon passes."

"But I wasn't *actually* punched."

"With every successful strike, puzzle solved or kill made in the game, the hoody delivers electrical pulses to your brain that release the right chemicals for you to feel the high," the Analyst tells me. "But if you get hit yourself, it triggers the pain nerves instead."

"The carrot and the stick!" Vince explains. "It's the ultimate gaming experience. Challenges, battles and Face-offs have real meaning and tension. Winning results in a much bigger high. It's addictive. The gamer never wants to lose – not at any cost."

"Don't worry," the Analyst says, as he pushes me back into the seat. "There's a pre-set Pain Limiter installed in every program."

My gut tightens as I allow the hoody to slip down. I blink and the forest returns.

"Back for more?" Kat-Ana laughs.

She picks a pink flower, sniffs it, then slips the blossom into her long brown hair. In a sweet voice, she begins to sing, "London Bridge is falling down, falling down, falling down ..."

I'm ready this time. I won't be fooled by her softly-softly approach. I drop into fighting guard.

Smiling, Kat-Ana launches herself at me. Her attack is brutal and I have to call on all my *tae kwon do* skills. I block her jab with my palm and come back with a back-fist. She drives a knee into my gut and I feel a bruising crunch. At the same time, my life-bar flashes 90%.

Kat-Ana attempts a roundhouse-kick. I shin-block it and drop into a spinning sweep-kick. I catch her by the ankles and knock her to the ground. A huge rush floods my body as Kat-Ana loses 20% of her life-bar.

"You've got skills for a newbie," admits Kat-Ana, flipping back to her feet. "But it won't save you."

She drives into me. I collapse under her power. Life-bar 75%. Pain flares round my body as she lands strike after strike. 60%. I manage to counter and force her to retreat across the fight zone. I even manage to land a few hits myself. For a moment, the high wipes out the pain. But she's too fast for me.

Slipping to my other side, Kat-Ana roundhouse kicks me. 45%. Then a kidney-punch drops me to my knees. 35%.

Before I can recover, Kat-Ana unsheathes her sword.

"NO!" I cry.

But it's too late. She slices off my head.

"KILLING STRIKE!"

I scream as white noise rips through me.

Then nothing. I'm back in the real world.

"Hmm ... Not bad," says Vince as I stumble out of Door 12, dazed and rubbing my neck. "New kombatants don't often survive more than a few seconds."

To my mind it felt like seconds. But the clock on the wall shows a plug-in time of over five minutes.

A bell rings. "That'll be lunch," Vince says. "This is where I say goodbye."

We salute Vince, and two guardians escort us back to the dining hall. The place is crammed with kid kombatants. I spot Kat-Ana in the line and go up to her.

"There was no need to cut my head off!" I protest. I can still feel a hot itch where the blade went through my avatar's neck.

"Don't be such a sore loser," she says, passing me a tray. "It's just a game. Anyway, with a face like yours, I was doing you a favour!"

Before I can think of a comeback she says, "You should try the sub-fish," then blows me a kiss and walks away. "Tastes like the real thing."

CHAPTER 8
The Catch

"Here you are, love," says the friendly guardian with a broad smile as she dumps an extra helping of sub-fish on my plate. "Looks like you could do with building up."

I thank her and wander round the hall looking for a seat. The Ginger Ninja sees me and slides along his bench to make space. I take the invite.

"I hear Kat-Ana gave you a haircut!" he sniggers, slurping at a cherry Synapse drink.

"At least my eyeballs stayed in my head," I shoot back.

Ginger Ninja laughs and rubs his still-red eyes.

"So how come she's got a weapon?" I ask, nodding at Kat-Ana on the other side of our table.

"It's a Mod," he says. "The more training sessions you do and Face-offs you win, the more points you earn. You can use your points to buy Mods and Power-Ups in the game. A samurai sword doesn't come cheap, though. You need a *lot* of points for that."

"What other gear can you get?" I ask.

Ginger Ninja grins. "Whatever your wicked heart desires! I got myself a set of exploding throwing stars. They do *big* damage. I'll show you if you're up for a Face-off."

"Sounds tempting," I say. But I'm not so sure I want to feel my body parts being blown off, VK-style.

Ginger Ninja cranes round to look at my tag.

"What sort of avatar name is Scott?" he asks.

"It's *my* name," I reply, wishing I could have thought of a decent tag.

Kat-Ana looks up. "I think it's good to keep a handle on reality. Spend too long in the game and you soon forget what's real."

"So what's your name?" I ask.

She smiles at me. "Kate."

I turn to the Ginger Ninja. "And yours?"

"I need no other name," says Ginger Ninja, pointing at his carrot top and then doing a karate chop in mid-air.

Kate rolls her eyes. "See what I mean? Bet he doesn't even remember what his real name is."

Ginger Ninja ignores her and takes another slurp of Synapse.

"So, Kate, what's the deal here?" I ask. "Test a few games and we get fed and housed?"

"Pretty much."

I look round at the hundreds of other kids tucking into their food. "All this seems too good to be true. What's the catch?"

"Haven't found it yet."

"But why so many testers?"

"Who cares?" says Ginger Ninja, forking more sub-fish into his mouth. "As long as I'm fed, I'll play. It beats the streets any day."

Kate picks up her tray. "I'll show you where to dump these."

I follow her to the recycling bins.

Kate glances round and waits for a stern-faced guardian to pass by. Then she leans in close and whispers. "There *is* a catch. VK's addictive. It's lethal."

"So why are you still playing?" I ask. All of a sudden, I have the feeling we're being watched.

"You've got to play the game to get out."

As the guardian strides over, Kate drops her tray down the chute.

"That's where the trays go," she says. She whispers as she walks away, "Take my advice. Never forget who you are."

CHAPTER 9
Trigger Time

The Analyst hands me my training report.

Performance – 5 out of 10.

Bruiser, a Brazilian ju-jitsu fighter, destroyed me in the last Face-off. My back still aches from where he power-kicked me.

After two months of gameplay, I've climbed into the upper ranks of the League. But now I'm struggling to keep my place there. And that's even with the Mod and the Power-Up that I've earned. The Mod is a pair of Kevlar arm-guards that block any blade. And the Power-Up is a single-use Mega-Punch that lets me do three times more damage with any strike.

None of that helped against Bruiser. Like Kat-Ana, he moves too fast for me to land an attack in the first place.

"What's up?" Ginger Ninja asks as I enter the Chill Zone and flop on a beanbag next to him and Kate.

"However hard I try, I keep getting beat to the Killing Strike," I admit.

Kate looks up from her avatar fashion e-mag. "Your skills are good," she says. "But you need to master Trigger Time."

I frown at her. "That's not in my feedback."

"That's cos the Analysts don't know about it," she says. "It's not an official part of the game. Come on, I'll show you."

"Hey, you promised to teach *me*!" Ginger Ninja complains.

"You're not ready for it," replies Kate, heading for the door.

My body protests at leaving the beanbag. After gaming for three hours straight, my brain hurts like a strained muscle. VK's a serious workout. Your mind *believes* your body's done all that fighting. By the end of the first week, I felt like I'd run a marathon then been mashed by a runaway MPV.

Even now I'm brain-fit, VK's still a drain. But I can't resist. I'm hooked.

We enter the Training Zone. There are no Analysts at the control module.

"It's Downtime," Kate explains. "We can still log on, though."

She presses a touch-screen and two PlayPod doors open.

"What's behind here?" I ask, going over to the "Restricted Access" door.

Kate shrugs. "The guardians don't like it when you snoop around."

"It might lead outside."

"Curiosity killed the rat," she says as I try the handle.

"Cat," I say. "You mean 'curiosity killed the cat'."

"Cat, rat, whatever," she says. "When you VK loads, words get jumbled up."

"It's locked, anyway," I say, and I leave the door.

We clamber into our PlayPods and boot up.

A shooting-range Arena blinks into life, complete with weapons. Kat-Ana's standing beside me.

"Take this," she says, and she passes me a handgun. Then she walks to the end of the range. "Shoot me," she says.

I don't want to raise the gun. I know it's only the gameworld, but it feels wrong. "Won't it hurt pretty bad?" I ask.

"Do it!"

I pull the trigger. BANG. With lightning speed, Kat-Ana bends to one side. Her body flickers as the bullet thuds into the target behind.

"But that's impossible!" I cry.

"Not in VK. This is a computer-created world implanted in your head. It's only impossible because you believe it is."

She hands me a suit of Kevlar armour. "Put this on, or else you'll feel beat up when we finish."

"You're going to shoot *me?*"

She nods. "To master Trigger Time, your brain has to work faster than the game can download into your head."

"Sounds hard," I say as she makes me stand before the target.

"It is. But if you concentrate hard enough, you can bend the rules of the game. Slow down virtual time." She takes aim at me. "Think of it like intense meditation. Focus on the gun, my every movement. See it all. Even before it happens."

I'm sweating now. The barrel is pointed at my chest. "But how will I know if I'm getting it right?"

"When you get it right, your opponent seems to attack in slow-mo. But you move at normal speed. That's when you can dodge or land any strike."

She fires.

I don't even see the bullet. But I feel the heavy slug thud into my chest. I get blown off my feet.

"Concentrate!" says Kat-Ana as she reloads.

Rubbing my bruised ribs, I get back up and focus on her again. She raises the gun and takes aim. She seems slower this time. But that could be my imagination.

BANG. The bullet catches my side like a battering ram and spins me round.

"Better," she says. "At least you moved this time."

The pain makes me focus. I centre my mind on Kat-Ana. I break down her every movement.

Hand rising. Finger on trigger. Muscle squeezing. Click of ignition. Flare of barrel. A low, long, rumbling bang. The bullet appearing. Flying through the air.

I shift to one side.

The slug passes me by.

Pierces the target.

With a sound like a thunderclap, time catches up. Sound and vision compress back to normal speed.

"Well done!" Kat-Ana calls. "Now you've done it once, it'll be much easier next time."

She presses her ESCAPE button and disappears.

The Arena blinks out.

As we head back to dinner, I ask, "It's a neat trick, but what if everyone's using Trigger Time?"

"You can't keep it up for more than a few seconds," Kate says. "It creates too much brain-strain. So you have to pick your moments."

"But now I know it, aren't you worried I'll beat you?"

"You won't get the chance," she replies, grinning. "I'm one Face-off from becoming an Elite Gamer. When I win, I'll be top of the League. Then I'm out of here. Special Projects! VK for real. The Crown. Fame and fortune, baby. Fame and fortune."

My mouth drops open. But not at her boasting.

Right in front of me, standing in the dinner line, is Shark.

CHAPTER 10
Blaze and Burn

I'm backed into a corner.

Shark advances on me, his fists raised.
I dodge his jab. Counter with a hook-punch. His
head rocks with the blow but he keeps up his
attack. His knee lands in my stomach.

As I gasp for breath, his axe-kick almost gets
me. His heel passes my head and slams into the
floor, where it shatters the tiles.

I kick him hard in the chest. He flies back
into the wall. I give him no time to recover. I
bear down on him, determined to finish the fight.

From out of nowhere, Shark pulls a Blazer.

"Blaze and burn time!" he sneers.

The pulse-blade slashes across my chest.
I jump back, but its laser edge rips into my skin.

Gloating, Shark rams the Blazer into me. I try to block, but it's too late. I feel the burn as the pulse-blade enters my stomach and I scream in pain as he twists it.

"That's for making me suffer another two months on those stinking streets!" he shouts.

Shark pulls the pulse-blade out. I can only watch as he goes for the Killing Strike. He raises the Blazer, his face ugly with fury. The pulse-blade glows orange in the light. Its laser arcs towards my neck.

I concentrate hard and see it all in slow-mo.

With the last of my energy, I roll to the side, Power-Up and use my Mega-Punch. My fist catches him bang on the temple. His eyes spin in his head like a slot machine. I've hit the jackpot.

"KILLING STRIKE!" booms the VK ringmaster.

The Arena shrinks to a dot and blinks out.

As I climb from my PlayPod, my stomach throbs where the virtual blade cut into me. But it soon fades under the amazing high of my win. I'm also buzzing from my first chance to use

Trigger Time in kombat. It's taken me two weeks of constant practice to perfect it.

Shark exits, his head in his hands. The loser. No addictive kick of winning for him.

As we go up for our feedback, he narrows his eyes and spits in my face.

"I don't know *how* you beat me. But I'll blaze you for real one of these days."

CHAPTER 11
Missing in Action

"Have you seen Kate?" I ask.

Ginger Ninja doesn't even look away from the big screen. It's VK Primetime. Destroy has climbed another place. To my dismay, he's just killed Spider, a *tae kwon do* fighter from Korea.

"Nah," says Ginger Ninja, stuffing a Zing bar into his mouth. "Not since she went training for the Face-off tomorrow."

I head down to the Training Zone, but Kate's not plugged in. She must have got an early night.

But she's still not around at breakfast. That worries me. I check out the dorms, the Training Zone and, last, the Chill Zone.

"Anyone seen Kate?"

I'm met with blank looks.

"Kat-Ana?" I repeat, irritated by how little they seem to care.

Shark flashes his razor grin at me. "Lost your girlfriend?"

"She's not my girlfriend," I snap. "What have you got to smile about anyway?"

"Nothing," replies Shark, a sly look in his eyes.

"I think Kat-Ana made it to Elite Gamer status," pipes up Vixen. She points to the leader-board.

Kate's name is no longer listed.

"Did you see the final Face-off?" I ask.

Vixen shakes her head.

"Who fought her? Did *anyone* see it?"

I'm greeted with silence. Kate's missing and no one cares. They're all too zoned out with VK. OK, a lot of kids pass through the Kombat system. But something's wrong here. Final Face-offs always draw a crowd in the Chill Zone.

"Won't she have gone to Special Projects?" Vixen asks.

"She'd have told me."

"That's girls for you!" says Ginger Ninja, rolling his eyes.

The only thing the guardians would say when I asked where Kat-Ana had gone was, "She must have qualified." Even the friendly one in the kitchen was no help.

Maybe I'm being paranoid. I just thought we were friends. That she'd at least say goodbye.

I watch VK Primetime over the next few days and keep a hopeful eye out for Kat-Ana in the Grand Arena League. But her tag doesn't appear.

"Hey, Scott," Vixen whispers as we line up for dinner a week later. "I hear Shark has it in for you."

I nod, trying not to give too much away.

"Rumour is, he's somehow got himself a Blazer," she said. "I'd watch your back if I were you."

I park myself beside Ginger Ninja, but I no longer feel like eating. Shark's sitting three tables over, slicing his sub-beef and veg.

Blaze and burn.

It's only a matter of time. I can't avoid him for ever.

I have to get out.

But how? The guardians make sure no one leaves the building.

This place is starting to feel more like a prison than a home.

Kate said the only way out is through the game. Seems, for the second time, that my very life depends upon it.

CHAPTER 12
Elite Gamer

"Congratulations," says the Analyst, his voice flat and bored. "Top of the League. You've made Elite Gamer."

I want to jump for joy. But I'm too tired.

Three weeks of solid VK has paid off. I'm going into Special Projects. Maybe I'll find out what's happened to Kate.

Whatever, it's a relief after playing cat-and-mouse with Shark every day. I've been avoiding him at all costs. Training all the time. Sticking to the dining hall and Chill Zone when they're packed with people. I make sure I'm never alone. I'm not in his dorm, but even at night I have to keep sharp.

Not easy, when my brain's so mashed with VK that I find it hard to remember who I am.

I head to the showers to freshen up before dinner.

As I'm getting changed into a clean kombat suit, I hear a threatening buzz. The orange glow of a Blazer pulse reflects off the lockers.

As I look round, I find the changing room has emptied.

Then Shark appears.

"No more games," he hisses. "This is for real."

I back towards the showers. There's only one way out. And Shark's between me and the door.

I grab my towel and wrap it round my hand. It might give me an extra second or two to get the Blazer off him, before the pulse-blade burns through my fingers.

Just as Shark goes to blaze me, a *swoosh* alerts us to an opening door. Shark turns off the Blazer as fast as he can and pockets the weapon.

"Scott!" a guardian barks. "Special Projects. Follow me."

I push past Shark, who's fuming. He's missed his final chance to blaze and burn me.

I'm out of here.

As the guardian leads me down the corridor, I spot Vixen in the Chill Zone and give her a wave.

I've no one else to say goodbye to. Now that Kat-Ana's not in the League, Ginger Ninja has made Elite Gamer at last. He beat Bruiser in his last Face-off this week.

The guardian leads me into the Training Zone.

Door 1 is open, the PlayPod primed. An Analyst is by its side, ready to plug me in.

"Is this Special Projects?" I ask, a bit confused.

The Analyst nods and straps me down.

"But isn't it at a different site?"

I'm worried Shark might get another chance to blaze me.

"Don't worry," the Analyst says. "You're not coming back."

Before I can protest, the hoody slips down.

A jolt of light. A gliding feeling.

I boot straight into a major battle.

CHAPTER 13
No Escape

The castle yard where I stand is over-run with kombatants. They fight tooth and nail against one another, till blood flows across the stone cobbles. It's carnage.

Multi-player kombat. Just like Primetime VK, where players plug in from around the world to fight for the Crown.

A samurai swordsman charges at me.

I block his *katana* blade with my arm. Then I kick him in the chest. As he clambers to his feet, I catch him with a spinning hook-kick across the jaw. He makes a wild swing with his sword, but my fist-punch to his head finishes him off. His life-bar blinks out.

The victory gives me a boost I badly need.

Then a fearsome Maori warrior jumps from the castle wall, roaring. His face is a swirl of black tattoos. In his hand he carries a great barbed spear.

His roaring battle chant sends a chill through my body.

He pounds his chest and snarls at me as he advances.

I power-kick him in the gut, but it has zero effect. His great slab of a fist smashes me in the face. I feel my nose break. My life-bar reads 80%.

My head rings with pain and my vision flashes red.

The warrior knees me hard in the side. I feel a rib crack. Pain shoots through me. 65%.

I stumble over the samurai's dead body and fall to the ground. The Maori warrior drives his spear into my stomach. I scream. The agony is overpowering.

What's happened to the Pain Limiter? The game never felt this bad before. Never this ... *real*.

My life-bar drops to 50%.

It's like I'm dying. 45%.

I stab and stab at the ESCAPE button on my belt.

Nothing happens. 40%.

The pain roars to a new high as the Maori warrior pulls out the spear. 35%.

In a last desperate attempt, I crawl away.

But the Maori warrior grabs me by my ankle and flings me into the castle wall. 25%.

The pain rises in my head, like a ball of fire.

I'm passing out now, still trying to press the button.

The Maori warrior roars at me as he raises his spear to deliver the Killing Strike.

But a kombatant in shorts and T-shirt jumps between us. Her samurai sword slices through him. His spear drops to the floor with his hands still attached. The word "critical" flickers on the warrior's life-bar before Kat-Ana finishes him off.

Kat-Ana sheathes her sword and begins to sing.

"London Bridge is falling down, falling down, falling down ..."

My vision breaks into pixels as the signal corrupts.

Kat-Ana slaps me hard in the face. "Stay with me."

"What did you do that for?" I yell. I'm confused and swimming in pain.

"You need to focus on being alive. And stop moaning. It's only a gameworld slap!"

She pulls me to my feet.

"We've got to get out of here," she says, dragging me in the direction of the drawbridge. "And stop pressing that stupid button. There is *no* escape."

CHAPTER 14
Reality Check

"There has to be some mistake," I gasp, as Kat-Ana makes me lie down on the floor of a cave.

Kat-Ana hands me a health pack. My wound heals in seconds. My life-bar climbs back to 75%.

"No mistake," she replies. "We're plugged into the Grand Arena."

I stare at her, stunned. The Grand Arena is the fighting world of VK2! A series of connected Battle Arenas where kombatants have to fight their way to the Crown.

"But I was supposed to go to Special Projects. I shouldn't be here."

"None of us should."

"You mean there are others?"

Kat-Ana nods.

I sit up and my head throbs. "It feels as if my brain's been fried."

"It has. You almost died back there," she points out.

"But this is just a game!"

"No. This is reality," Kat-Ana says.

"I don't understand."

"Yesterday, when I left you to go training –"

I interrupt. "Kate, you've been gone four weeks."

Her mouth drops open in shock. "You lose all track of time in VK," she explains.

She slumps down next to me. A faraway look enters her eyes and she begins to hum "London Bridge" again.

"Are you all right?" I ask.

Kat-Ana snaps out of her daze. "Sorry. Anyway, when I left you I headed to the Training Zone. The Restricted Access door was open. I saw them wheel a boy out on a stretcher. The top of his head was black and smoking. The

Analysts said the hoody was too powerful. It was the second Burn Out that week."

A cold chill runs through my body at her words.

"The VK2 program demands too much of our brains," she adds. "They blow like a fuse."

"Are you saying if we die in the Grand Arena, we die in the real world too?"

"It would seem so."

"But why didn't you tell anyone?"

She shrugs. "I tried to, but they sealed the doors before I could escape. Strapped me into the PlayPod. The next thing I knew, I was fighting for my life in the Grand Arena. My ESCAPE button had been disabled."

I punch the wall in anger. "So we're just lab rats for Vince Power!"

"Pretty much. But we're not just testing the game. We are the game."

"What?"

"You know what the advert says. WHERE EVERY ENEMY HAS A MIND OF ITS OWN."

I nod, but I don't want to believe what she's about to tell me.

"We're the enemy, Scott. That's why Vince Power needs so many kids to feed his system. And now that we're part of the game, every VK2 player in the world is out to kill us!"

CHAPTER 15
Back Door

"We must keep moving," says Kat-Ana, peering over her shoulder with a frown.

I follow her gaze down the long, deserted road behind us.

"Why?" I ask, sitting on a rock to rest. My stomach's still sore from the attack.

"VK2 will send Skirmishers. Electro-bots to drive us towards the next Arena. We need to avoid trouble until your life-bar is back at 100%. You'll need all of it, if you're gonna survive."

My bar pulses green. 89%. "Give me a minute," I say.

I can tell she wants to push on, but Kat-Ana gives in and sits down next to me. She starts to sing again. "London Bridge is falling down, falling down ..."

"What's with the nursery rhyme?" I ask.

She stops and blinks, as if she's forgotten where she is. "It keeps me connected to the real world. Reminds me of my dad. He used to sing it to me as a child." Tears run down her face. "It's the only thing that keeps me going," she sobs.

It's strange to see her cry, in her tough warrior princess form. But I know that the real Kate lies behind the avatar. I put my arm round her, hoping it's an OK thing to do. Hoping it's some comfort.

Kat-Ana wipes her eyes. "Most kid kombatants you meet in VK2 have forgotten who they are," she says. "The game's taken over their minds. There is no other world to them."

The thought of becoming lost for ever in VK sends a shudder of terror down my spine. It makes me even more determined. "There must be some way of escape," I say.

My words work some magic and Kate is Kat-Ana again, her eyes blazing with strength. "My dad was an IT consultant," she says. "He said programmers always leave a back door in their code. A way in and out. That's what I was looking for in the castle."

"Any luck?"

"I found a clue scratched on a wall in the castle dungeon. I don't think it's meant to be part of the game. It said –

Between Heaven and Earth lies ESCAPE,
Nearby the Crown seals your fate.

"The only place I haven't looked yet is the Citadel," she says. She points into the distance, where a number of towers poke through the clouds. "That's where the Crown is. But we'll have to fight our way through every VK player to get there."

"Who dares wins," I reply. My life-bar is now at 100%.

In the distance, a whirring electric hum speeds towards us.

"Time to go," says Kat-Ana. She jumps to her feet. "That's the Skirmishers."

CHAPTER 16
The Forest

Three gleaming metal droids roar over the hill. Their electric spikes crackle with sparks and force us off the road and down a narrow track into a forest. We just make it to the tree line when the Skirmishers turn back and leave us.

"Stay alert," Kat-Ana says. "That means VK players are ahead."

As we trek deeper into the forest, the sunlight gives way to a gloomy darkness. We enter a clearing. It's too still.

"An Arena," whispers Kat-Ana. "Let's cross before anyone else gets here."

We're half way across when a shadow drops from the trees.

Kat-Ana draws her sword and turns to face the tiny assassin. He wears a black cloak and a mask, but a curl of red hair pokes out at his neck.

"Ginger Ninja!" I exclaim, pleased to see our friend.

He stares at me, his brow creased in distrust.

Then he throws a gleaming star.

Kat-Ana shoves me aside. The metal star strikes a tree trunk behind us and explodes. Burning wood flies everywhere.

"Ginger Ninja. It's us! Scott and Kate!" I scream as we run for cover.

"He doesn't recognise us," shouts Kat-Ana, diving behind a rock.

Another tree bursts into flames above our heads.

As Ginger Ninja throws a third star, more kombatants enter the Arena. A Special Forces soldier attacks him from behind. Ginger Ninja stands no chance.

I dash out to save my friend, driving the soldier back with a flying kick. Ginger Ninja thanks me by punching me in the face.

"Don't fight me," I plead as his strikes rain down on me. I block his attacks, but don't dare fight back.

"But that's the whole point of VK!" Ginger Ninja replies. He lands an evil side-kick that sends me flying across the clearing.

I bang into a tree and slump to the ground. My life-bar flashes 70%.

Just as Ginger Ninja is about to follow up with his Killing Strike, a warrior monk attacks him. Ginger Ninja disappears in the swirl of combat.

I feel a hand grab my arm and turn to defend myself.

It's Kat-Ana. "Come on!" she hisses.

"But what about Ginger Ninja?"

"We can't help him now. He's lost to the game." She begins to cut a path through the seething mass of fighters. "We must get to the Citadel before the same happens to us!"

CHAPTER 17
The Citadel

"There it is!" Kat-Ana exclaims as we burst out of the forest.

The Citadel hangs in the sky, chained to the ground by a stone stairway.

The fight out has been bloody and messy. My life-bar hovers below 40%, Kat-Ana's at 50%. We share the last of her health packs, but afterwards we're only at 70% each.

We know the other kombatants aren't far behind, and so we sprint up the flight of steps. Half way to the top, I hear the stone begin to crack. Slabs of rock peel away and spiral towards the ground, hundreds of metres below.

"Go! Go! GO!" I urge.

We take the steps two at a time, the staircase collapsing behind us as we run.

The higher we climb, the harder it is to stay ahead of the falling steps.

Just metres from the Citadel, the floor beneath Kat-Ana's feet disappears. Screaming, she drops like a stone.

I snatch for her outstretched hand.

Somehow I get a grip. Glad that my avatar is strong enough, I pull Kat-Ana to safety.

We collapse against the Citadel's door, breathless and shaking.

"That was *too* close," I gasp as we watch the stone stairway reconstruct itself – a deadly VK trap.

"Thank you," Kat-Ana says, kissing me with relief.

I stare at her, a bit taken aback.

Suddenly Kat-Ana realises what she's done. She blushes.

"It's only a virtual kiss!" she blusters. "Come on, we've got to keep moving."

She strides over to the great gate and shoves it open.

I smile to myself and follow her inside.

We enter a huge hall. The final Arena.

Flags line the walls and a blazing VK emblem hangs over a throne at the other end. A shiny marble floor stretches before us, a vast mosaic map of the world laid into its surface. At the centre, on a glass pedestal, I see the gleaming Crown.

"Fame and fortune," Kat-Ana breathes, staring at the prize.

"Forget that!" I say, grabbing her. "We must escape. Remember the clue."

She nods slowly. *"Between Heaven and Earth lies ESCAPE."*

I point to a small, plain wooden door in the far corner of the room. On the floor is the world map. Above the door is a carving of an angel from Heaven.

CHAPTER 18
The Crown

"It really is a back door," Kat-Ana says in surprise.

I make a move towards it, but she yanks me back.

"Another trap!" she warns as a great curving blade shoots past, inches from my face.

Six golden blades now swing across the hall like massive pendulums of death. Their razor-sharp edges whistle as they slice through the air.

"We'll have to time our crossing perfectly," Kat-Ana says.

We take a deep breath and step out into the Arena. It's hard to tell when to move as the blades keep changing speed and direction.

"Behind you!" I shout.

Kat-Ana rolls out of the way of a blade. I'm driven forwards by a second scythe. I leap past the next two and make a dash for the door. I'm almost there when I realise Kat-Ana's still in the middle of the Arena.

She's heading for the glass pedestal. Reaching for the Crown.

"No, leave it!" I shout.

"But this is the ultimate prize," replies Kat-Ana, like a person in a dream.

Her eyes are glazed over. She's lost to the game.

Nearby the Crown seals your fate.

"Kate, remember who you are!" I scream.

But she's not listening any more.

"LONDON BRIDGE IS FALLING DOWN, FALLING DOWN ..." I sing at the top of my voice, prancing around like a court jester to get her attention.

The nursery rhyme breaks her trance just in time. That's when the gates to the hall burst open and Destroy strides in.

He has come to claim the Crown.

"Run!" I shout.

But it's too late. With one great leap, Destroy avoids the blades and blocks Kate's path.

She tries to skirt round him, but he slams her with a hook-punch. Kate is thrown back against the pedestal and crumples to the floor.

Destroy stands over her limp body and raises his fists for the Killing Strike.

"No!" I scream.

Ignoring the swinging blades, I throw myself at him. I land a powerful flying kick. But Destroy seems not even to feel the impact. He blasts past my guard and palm-strikes me in the chest.

My life-bar flashes 60%. Pain flares as I feel a rib break.

I try to fight back, but Destroy is too strong.

50%.

My punches and kicks bounce off him. It's like hitting a brick wall. 45%.

He drives me towards the rear wall and I'm almost sliced by a passing blade. He catches me with a punishing upper cut. 30%.

My vision breaks into pixels. I'm on the verge of blacking out. 25%. Destroy prepares to deliver his trademark Skull Crusher blow.

In a last-ditch attempt, I recall Kat-Ana's training and focus all my brain-power on Destroy's every move.

His muscles ripple. His fists clench. He growls deep in his throat as he brings them down.

Behind him, a scythe slows its swing.

I've entered Trigger Time.

Destroy's fists almost grind to a halt as I move out of their path. Then I select my Mega-Punch and use it to hammer Destroy in the gut. He staggers backwards in slow-mo. Right into the path of the blade.

The strain of Trigger Time is too much for me and the game speeds back up. Destroy's scream rises in pitch like a jet engine taking off.

Though my win awards me a boost, I'm still weak. 40%. But I'm glad to see Kate's recovered. She gets back to her feet as two more kombatants enter the Arena.

"Kate! This way!" I plead.

"Kate?" she says, shooting me a confused look. "I'm the warrior princess, KAT-ANA!"

And then she draws her sword and charges at the new arrivals.

CHAPTER 19
Face-off

"NO!" I shout, dashing after Kate.

I won't lose her to VK. Not after everything we've been through.

But a kombatant in a black leather jacket and shades jumps in front of me.

"Time for our final Face-off!" he snarls.

"Shark?"

As he grins, I see that his avatar's teeth are filed into sharp points. "It's BLAZER to you!" he laughs.

He makes two fists and two pulse-blades burst into life from his knuckles. A high-level Mod.

With the speed of a panther, he slashes at me. The lasers rake across my bare chest, burning my flesh.

I stagger away, blood pouring from the wounds. 35%.

He comes at me again. As I block his thrust, a Blazer passes within a hair's breadth of my face. I fight back with a front-kick, a hard jab and a spinning back-fist that connects with his jaw. Shark grunts in pain as two teeth fly out.

While I have the advantage, I select my Mega-Punch.

But nothing happens.

I must have used my last charge against Destroy.

"Blaze and burn time!" growls Shark, coming at me in a wild blur of pulse-blades and flying kicks.

I duck and weave. As I retreat, I almost get cut in half by a swinging blade. I look to Kat-Ana for help, but she's deep in brutal kombat with a Shaolin monk.

My only hope is Trigger Time. But I've never done it twice in the same game. There's a chance I'll Burn Out.

With no other choice, I focus on Shark's every move.

His attacks still come fast and furious. He catches me in the head with a roundhouse-kick. 30%.

Dazed as I am, my brain burning with the strain, I try again.

This time, the Arena slows.

I escape Shark's laser fist and launch a knife-hand strike to his neck.

Just as my hand reaches its target, Shark speeds up. A pulse-blade cuts across my arm. I scream out in agony. 20%. He kicks me in the chest and I'm sent spinning into the central pedestal. 15%.

VK compresses back to normal time with a thunderclap of sound and vision.

"Think you're the only one who knows *that* trick?" Shark says with a laugh.

I'm too shocked to move. He's mastered Trigger Time!

The pain in my head rages now like a forest fire as Shark grabs me by the throat. He clenches his other fist and its pulse-blade burns bright orange as he levels it with my right eye.

I'm going to die – for *real*!

"Don't you ... want ... fame and fortune?" I splutter, nodding at the Crown.

Shark looks up and sees Kat-Ana, bloody but alive, heading for the pedestal.

"Not before I slice you into shark bait!" he spits, and tosses me into the path of a swinging blade.

As Shark and the wounded Kat-Ana battle for the prize, I struggle to my feet.

The blade arcs towards me.

I realise there's only one way to save her.

I dive for the door.

CHAPTER 20
PlayPods

I blink as the hoody comes off.

I rip at the velcro straps and clamber out.

My body feels bruised and battered, and my head throbs.

There's a drip in my arm. I yank it free.

As I glance round, I'm completely confused. I'm not in the Training Zone. I've been moved to a low-lit warehouse. For a moment, I can't believe my eyes. Rows upon rows of PlayPods stretch into the distance. Kids are plugged into every one.

There must be thousands of them.

Each pod has a screen with the player's tag, Arena, life-bar, vital signs in real life and their date of entry into the game.

I have to find Kate. Get her out before Shark kills her.

I hurry down my row, looking for a date four weeks before mine. As I pass one pod, I catch the sickening smell of burnt hair.

I pray it's not her. I check the screen. Thankfully, the date's too early.

Then I find her PlayPod. She's still fighting for the Crown. But her life-bar is at 20%.

I call up the menu. 15%.

I search for an escape option. 10%.

Her body starts to fit within the pod. 5%.

I find the icon and press ESCAPE. The screen freezes at 1%.

I pull back her hoody. Her eyes focus on me, seem to spark blue, then fade.

"Scott, *never* forget who you are," she says, with a weak smile. "I won't forget you."

Her head lolls to one side. The PlayPod emits a long droning beep. Her vital signs zero out.

I choke back tears. On the street, friends are few and far between. It's survival that matters most. Kate was my first *real* friend.

But I don't get time to grieve.

All of a sudden, the lights come on.

I duck down as two Analysts head towards the pod with the Burned Out kid inside.

"What a week!" one kid moans. "Three in a row. We'll have to promote more kids to Elite Gamer status."

As he passes my empty PlayPod, he shouts, "Hey, a player's unplugged!"

Then he slams a red emergency button and an alarm blares out.

I run.

CHAPTER 21
The Greater Good

I weave between the PlayPods, heading for the nearest exit.

I force it open, enter a stairwell and begin to climb. I bound up two steps at a time, but I'm not as strong as my avatar. By the sixth flight, I'm out of breath. Every door so far's been locked.

I hear voices and footsteps clattering up the stairs.

Forcing myself to go on, I reach the top floor. To my relief, this door opens.

I burst out onto a roof garden and the cold night air hits my face.

Street Screens blaze across the city. A glass dome rises before me, and below it I can see the Orphans' Home dining hall. I hammer on the glass, trying to warn the other kombatants of their fate. But no one can hear me above Primetime VK.

The shouts of my followers are getting louder.

I dash to the edge of the roof. But the other buildings are too far away. Below in the darkness, an inky strip of the city's river reflects the glow of Street Screens.

"I wouldn't, if I were you," a silky smooth voice advises me.

Vince Power comes out of his rooftop penthouse, drink in hand, and he flashes his pearly white smile at me.

"It would be a waste to lose such an impressive kombatant," he says. "How *ever* did you beat Destroy's Skull Crusher?"

I don't answer. Trigger Time must remain a secret.

"You know VK *kills!*" I rage, thinking of Kate.

Vince Power shrugs, not bothered. "It's just a glitch in the game. Only seems to affect the kids who play."

"But why don't you fix it?"

"That would take time. And I need you kids in the game. You feed VK2's processors. Your minds are like microchips, powering enemy avatars. For some reason your death in the game causes overloading. A Burn Out."

"You're worse than the devil!" I exclaim.

"I'm *not* evil!" he snaps, his smile gone.

"But you're killing kids."

"I've always believed in the greatest good for the greatest number. VK not only provides entertainment for millions, it's solved many of this world's problems. Reduced crime. Taken kids off the streets. Provided this city's only Orphans' Home. It's even good for the environment! A few deaths is a small price to pay."

"Murder is *never* a small price to pay," I cry.

"Yet gamers round the world get a kick out of killing in the gameworld," Vince counters. "And besides, some pay more, a lot more, for the privilege of killing for *real*."

"But it's not *supposed* to be real."

"Is it really that different? The players all *want* to kill, whether someone actually dies or not."

I'm stumped by his argument. He's a good politician, always ready with his answers.

"We could do with a gamer of your ability," he says, all smooth and smiling again. "Together we might be able to fix the Burn Out issue."

"Never," I reply as two Analysts appear. They are both carrying electric stun guns. "I'd rather die free on the streets than live like a slave in VK."

"I'm sorry to hear that," says Vince. He nods to the two Analysts.

They advance on me, guns raised.

I take a last glance over the lip of the roof.

"You'll never survive the fall," Vince says.

"WHO DARES WINS!" I cry ... and I leap into the darkness.

CHAPTER 22
Log-off

Vince was wrong.

I did survive.

But now I'm on the run.

With a secret no one believes.

Vince Power *must* be stopped.

If you're reading this, be warned ...

TO PLAY IS TO DIE!

Our books are tested
for children and young people by
children and young people.

Thanks to everyone who consulted on
a manuscript for their time and effort in
helping us to make our books better
for our readers.